For Firoozeh

All inquiries should be addressed to
Bentnose Books
At bentnosebooks@yahoo.com

With many thanks to my husband, Saeid,
for urging me to create a Norooz book for our daughter,
his creative ideas,
and his arduous efforts in production!

Gala
and her
Friends
Celebrate
Norooz

by
Karen McCormick

Soon it will be Spring and the new year will begin! Gala Seeb and her brothers and sisters are dressed in new clothes for the Norooz party.

Gala is so excited–she can't wait for the first moment of Spring and the party to celebrate it.

Seeb is the Farsi word for apple

Suddenly Gala is worried. She has asked her friend Maya Mahi, the goldfish, to come to the party with her. But Maya is nowhere to be found!

So she runs over to Sedrik Seer to learn if he has seen her friend Maya.

Sedrik is chatting with the other garlics and his purple flower friend Hyacinth. They are just about to leave for the party.

Seer is the Farsi word for garlic

"Have you seen Maya?" little Gala asks.

"No," replies Sedrik. "Hyacinth, have you seen Maya today?"

"No, I haven't, but maybe you should look in her bowl," Hyacinth replies. "I am sure that she won't miss the party! I'll be there, too, as Sedrik's guest."

"Great—I'll see you there!" says Gala. "I am sorry that I can't stay and talk, but I have to find Maya!"

As Gala leaves, Sammy Samanoo rolls into her. He is dressed in a shiny silver bowl. His tummy is all jiggley like a round brown pudding, and he laughs as he says, "Excuse me Gala, I didn't see you. I am sorry I bumped into you!"

He can see that Gala is worried. "Why are you so sad, little apple?" he asks.

"Because I can't find my friend Maya," Gala replies.

"Oh my," says Sammy, "let's go see Sarah Sabzeh. Maybe she knows where Maya is."

Samanoo is the Farsi word for sweet wheat germ pudding

Soon Sammy and Gala see Sarah Sabzeh. She is combing her lovely green tresses up tall and straight. A gaggle of beautifully colored eggs are helping her wrap a bright red ribbon around her waist.

Sabzeh is the Farsi word for green sprouts

"Hello Sarah," says Gala.
"You look beautiful."

"Thank you," replies Sarah, "I am wearing
my best ribbon for the first day of Spring.
My friends are helping me with it."

"You look troubled Gala Seeb, you should be happy today! What is the matter?" Sarah asks.

"I can't find my friend, Maya," Gala answers. "She is supposed to go with me to the Norooz party. Have you seen her?"

"No, but I am sure you will find her—you should ask the senjeds," says Sarah. "They always seem to know what is going on."

**Minutes later Gala finds the senjeds
with several bright and shiny gold coins.
They are practicing the poems they will
recite at the celebration.**

Senjed is the Farsi word for a small brown dried fruit

"Hello Gala, why are you in such a hurry?" asks Simin Senjed.

"I am looking for Maya Mahi. We are going to the party together. Have you seen her?" asks Gala.

"No, I haven't. Let me ask the coins." Simin turns to the coins and asks, "Has anyone seen Gala's goldfish friend, Maya?"

"Yes," answers the nearest coin, "I am sure I saw her in front of the gate to the party."

"Thanks!" says Gala, as she runs off in the direction of the party.

"Oops!" says Somerset Somagh, as Gala bumps into him spilling some of the deep purple powder. "What's your hurry my fine red friend?"

"I am looking for Maya," responds Gala. "I hope I didn't spoil your outfit, Somerset!"

"No, don't worry Gala," he says. "I can easily dust myself off and be as good as new. Go, run and find Maya. No one wants to be late for the celebration.

"Thanks Somerset, I'll see you at the the party." And Gala runs once more.

Somagh is the Farsi word for ground sumac berries

Soon Gala spots Sid Serkeh surrounded by sweets and cookies, each with a small scarf to make Sid's cruet gleam.

"Hello, my sweet Gala, where are you running to so fast?" asks Sid Serkeh.

"I am going to the party with my friend Maya Mahi. I am running to find her!" she replies.

"Then run Gala, run!" calls Sid.

Serkeh is the Farsi word for vinegar

"You found me!" calls out Maya.

Gala turns around to see her best friend looking back at her with a great big smile.

"Where were you?" asks Gala.

"Here! You said 'meet me at the gate'!" laughs Maya.

"No, I said 'meet me and don't be late'!" giggles Gala.

"Oh!!" they both laugh together.

"I am so glad I found you!" says Gala.

"So am I! Now we can go have fun together—let's go!!" says Maya.

As they enter the room for the celebration, the Book of Wisdom welcomes them.

"Hello Gala Seeb," says the book, "You are the first of the seven "S's" that I invited to the party. I am glad that you brought along your friend, the goldfish!"

Gala and Maya look into the room, beautifully lit by two tall candles. The light is reflected by a very large mirror in the middle of the hall. Soon it will also reflect all of the other invited "S's" and their friends.

Soon all the friends arrive.

They say 'hello' and greet each other.

Can you find all 7 S's?

"Let's take a picture," laughs Gala as they all settle down at the Haft Seen table.

At the first moment of Spring everyone cheers.

"Ayd-e shoma mobarak," says Gala as she gives Maya a hug and a kiss.

"Happy New Year," says Maya. "You are my best friend today and always."

HAPPY NOROOZ

For Parents:

In the Iranian tradition, Norooz is the first day of spring and the beginning of the new year. It begins at the first moment of the spring equinox, usually occurring on or around March 21st. Many other cultures around the world also celebrate Norooz.

The special Norooz table is called Sofreh-e Haft Seen. Sofreh literally means "table cloth". "Haft" means "seven" in Farsi, and seven items are always part of the table. All of these items begin with the letter "S", and "seen" is "S" in Farsi.

These seven items welcome spring and offer good wishes for the new year. Together they symbolize rebirth, health, persistence, prosperity, joy, patience, and beauty. The seven traditional items are:

- *Seeb is apple*
- *Seer is garlic*
- *Samanoo is a sweet creamy pudding made from wheat germ*
- *Sabzeh are green sprouts, often wheat or lentil sprouts*
- *Senjed is a small dried fruit that looks similar to a date*
- *Somagh is ground sumac berries*
- *Serkeh is vinegar*

Other items are often included on the Sofreh-e Haft Seen. Generally a goldfish, a hyacinth, gold coins and colored eggs are present. A mirror reflects lighted candles. A book of wisdom and special sweets are also customary.

Families gather together at the Sofreh-e Haft Seen, awaiting the first moment of the spring equinox (saw'at-e tahveel). Many wear new clothes for this special occasion. Elder family members often read from a holy book, recite poems, or tell stories. At the first moment of spring, best wishes are shared for the new year with each other—"Ayd-e shoma mobarak". The children receive gifts from their elders. Sweets and fruits are served. For the next twelve days friends and family visit each other to celebrate the new year. The thirteenth day after Norooz is called Seezdah Bedar, meaning "getting rid of the thirteenth day". On this day friends and family meet at a park to picnic and play. A common ritual at the end of the day is to throw away the sabzeh from the Haft Seen, getting rid of the bad omens collected in the previous days.

Ayd-e shoma mobarak!

Made in the USA
San Bernardino, CA
17 March 2018